THE HAMPSHIRE COLLECTION

An anthology of poems and short stories by Hampshire writers

Edited by Tim Saunders

Tim Saunders Publications   tsaunderspubs.weebly.com

TS
Tim Saunders Publications

Copyright © 2022 Contributors

All rights reserved

No part of this book may be reproduced, or stored in a retrieval system, or transmitted in any form or by any means, electronic, mechanical, photocopying, recording, or otherwise, without express written permission of the publisher.

Cover design: Beautiful bluebells on a woodland walk in the grounds of The Vyne, National Trust property near Basingstoke by Maria Ellis from Odiham, nr Hook, England. www.inspiredbycolour.co.uk
Library of Congress Control Number: 2018675309

FOREWORD

Initially this book was just a little seed of an idea that has quietly been germinating and has now flourished into this extremely satisfying anthology. It is a wonderful celebration of the creativity that exists in the beautiful county of Hampshire, England. During this project I have made 20 new friends that have created a rather special writing group and I hope to work on future projects with them. This book would be nothing without these very special people.

It feels quite apt to call this precious book of traditional poetry and short stories The Hampshire Collection. Readers will discover poetry and fiction covering many situations in life that we can all relate to as well as a sprinkling of fantasy and horror thanks to Arron Williams, which ought to hold the attention. There is some welcome and refreshing humour, too, which can be hard to write - especially these days - but is certainly rewarding to read.

Renowned Hampshire artist Maria Ellis has supplied the stunning front cover of bluebells at The Vyne; a delightful painting set in the grounds of this large country estate.

Thanks must go to the county's newspapers and magazines: The Hampshire Chronicle, Southern Daily Echo, Romsey Advertiser, Hampshire Life, Forum Publications, Discover magazine and Itchen Valley Forum, who all kindly spread the word about this exciting project. The result has been a steady trickle of poems and stories to my inbox and it has been an absolute pleasure to read each and every one.

All the contributors, including myself, are fortunate to live in this peaceful part of the world. However, when I started to compile this book, war was declared on Ukraine and so I have felt compelled to include a poem about this devastating invasion on the edge of Europe. A poem by Mark Rickenbach reminds us of its similarities with the Second World War.

Now that the rigorous selection process is over, I would like to share the results with you. This really is a book to cherish.

Tim Saunders
Editor
April 2022

POETRY
concise communication

RAYMOND ANDERSON

Raymond Anderson lives in Bishops Waltham, Hampshire. He has been involved in fine art for 55 years and has been writing seriously for the past two decades.

Bring

Bring me the hills, the valleys and streams,
Which enfold this pleasant land.
Give me the lark, the rook and the kite
That climbs and sweeps the lowering skies.
Let drive the rain, the mist and sheep
Through pastures green that stretch beyond
The maddening hype, the preening sties.

Raymond Anderson

Recalibrate

Of course I could curl up
In a foetus of self-pity
And waste time in blame.
Because they wish to destroy
Doesn't mean to say
I have to play their game.
I can recalibrate my heart,
Shake the monkey off my back.
Simply alter course,
Change tack.

Raymond Anderson

Time

He cannot fully recall what beset him,
But whatever it was rest assured
Jealousy, resentment and humiliation
All supplied significant measure.
He was shiftless, shapeless, hopeless and helpless,
Falling back among the barbs, banter and balsam
That rotated at the centre of his soul.
Borne on his shield from the field of passion,
In his heart lodged a dart called despair.
Now that Cupid's war had left him stricken,
She absolved herself from all responsibility
By simply saying: she still loved him.
Occasionally she would visit to assess
The hold she still had over him.
A state visit from a former love is hard to bear,
Bringing new sorrow in the train of old
Yet he was not eager to trade reproaches.
Instead he would sit scrutinised
Sifting through his grief,

Watching destiny shiver.
She did not say much,
But what was there to say?
What part of his psyche could he cope with anyway?
Her reserve showed no particular eloquence
Although her eyes missed nothing,
Too late he saw the pictures that kept her on his wall.
Now he would need time to assemble his emotions
It was time that saw the passing of passion,
Time understood necessity.
Time healed.

Raymond Anderson

SALLY BOURKE

Sally Bourke was a nurse for 54 years. She started writing poems when she was working as a community nurse. "After a day of supporting the sick and dying, I found writing therapeutic," says Sally, who has three daughters. She lives in "a delightful village" 10 miles from Winchester.

Honey I'm home

Drunk, came home at half past three
Can't find the lock, can't fit the key

Bangs and kicks, rattles and knocks
Even pees through the letterbox

She is in the hallway frozen with fear
Afraid to breathe in case he should hear

She opens the door with practice skill
Wedging herself against the sill

Door in front of her pulled up tight
So he can't hit her, start a fight

She waits until she thinks he has gone
Slumped in the armchair with the telly on

The door she closes without a sound
But he's behind her when she turns around

He grabs her hair and pulls her near
Puts his lips close to her ear, 'Thought you'd escaped, did you my dear?'

Sally Bourke

In my dreams

Walking by the river at early dawn
Bare feet soothed by the dew on the lawn
Expensive ball gown tattered and torn

Hold this memory to my heart
Years from now when I'm an old fart

I'll close my eyes and imagine this scene
Relive it again in my dreams
You don't think I was ever young, old and wrinkled, bent and glum

I danced all night, drank my fill
In my teens they invented the pill
Sitting in the sun nodding my head,

You keep checking to see if I'm dead

But I am dreaming, far away holding my children
Watching them play

Sally Bourke

LYNDSAY BARRETT

Lyndsay Barrett lives in Gosport, Hampshire where she grew up. Her main passion is writing and she is currently editing her science fiction novel. Lyndsay also writes short stories and when she feels inspired, poetry. An avid reader and writer from a very young age, Lyndsay also enjoys learning foreign languages and in 2021 passed her Dutch GCSE through home learning.

Torn

The breeze is fresh;
On the morning dew;
With the sun in the sky;
I think only of you.

Within my heart;
A lover's delight;

Until you leave;
Day becomes night.

The tears will come;
An eternal river;
The night is cold;
I can only shiver.

Here you will remain,
I want you to stay;
Until the next time;
When you are sent away.

Lyndsay Barrett

JILLY BOWLING

Jilly Bowling lives in Winchester and first started writing poetry when she was 12. "I can be inspired by anything at all," says Jilly, who was born in Lancashire in 1973. She grew up in Shaw, a small cotton mill town between Oldham and Rochdale and attended the Bluecoat School, Oldham and Crompton House School, Shaw.

The Lake
Inspired by Rooksbury Mill Lake, Andover

Wandering by the lakeside, and beauty I can see
The creatures that all live here, come up to visit me
Curious are the swans, alongside their babies follow
As songs can be heard from robin, blackbird, tit and swallow

So many different animals, are seen here every day
Some stay for summer and wintertime and others fly away

To return back here in springtime, when newly ones are born
To greet us all with precious song every single day at dawn

As I continue along my way, I see who spies on me
Ladybirds, and dragonflies and cormorants in the tree
And many find the otters but they're hiding somewhere near
They have nothing to be scared of, and nothing from me to fear

I even saw the lakeside cat, who followed me to talk
We chatted along the well-worn paths, as we carried on our walk
He then went on his way, where he went, I'll never know
But I am glad he came to see me, before he had to go

If you should pass along this way, and visit this beautiful place
Please look after our wildlife, and our lakeside open space
For the animals here who we enjoy, to see every single day
Will give their love back to us, in their own little unique way

Jilly L Bowling

Shades and Shadows
based on a true story and about the ghost of a lady at Bramshill House, which is now the Police Training College in Hampshire

Beneath the moon and a Christmas night
The windows flicker as passes a light
The light of a candle held by she
Who will walk the hall for eternity

In years gone by, she lived by the side
Of a Yorkshireman, she was to be his bride
On the night of her wedding, a game was begun
She wouldn't be found till the rise of the sun

That rise of the sun was fifty years long
That morning the birds broke with their song

A song that was mourning the death of the bride
As in a chest at long last, she was found trapped inside

In her hand the sprig of mistletoe lay
As fresh as it was from that fateful day
Still wearing her dress from the first day as his wife
Curled up in the chest that had taken her life

Bramshill House is where our lady will stay
Say 'Hello' to her, as you pass on your way
Our lady will pass you with a smile on her face
And you may hear her pass from the rustle of lace.

Jilly L Bowling

A Christmas Past

Long years have passed, and I sit and I think
Memories that fill my head from days
Cold winter times, with family around me
No longer the table shall fill with their beings

A time of joy, when a child I was
As love circled like warmth from the fire
Flames danced like a ballet of light
As I stared into what was never ending love

The fire was deep, like my memory is now
As words were said around me
Nothing was heard, but the crackling of the flames
To return to hear the words I missed, I wish I could

But time moves on and people leave us
Older the years, like us they mature
We cannot stay in the warmth of the fire
That now in the grate, is ashes nothing more

But we one day soon, will again be with them
The people, the warmth, the fire shall warm again
The souls, of myself and those who I miss
And Christmas past, will be our forever Christmas present.

Jilly L Bowling

Brighton Pier
The Brighton Palace Pier, commonly known as Brighton Pier,
was intended as a replacement for the Chain Pier, which
collapsed in 1896 during construction of the new pier

As she stood so very proud, there for all to see
We thought she would be standing there, for all eternity
But the power that took her to the depths, never to rise again
Time and tide do not wait for anyone, women, piers and men

As many feet have enjoyed her boards, looking out to sea
The people who have wandered, just like you and me
Walking upon water, with children safe in hands
Wandering over the ocean, far out away from sands

The excited laughter of others, as they
wade trousers rolled to knee
Hearing shouts of fishermen, as they bring in the evening tea
Cries from younger ones as their sand castles are taken away
To be brought back with tomorrows tide,
for another fun building day

Ice cream and rock, maybe cockles and winkles for a snack
Little children enjoying rides upon a donkey's back
Jingles and jangles as bells ring out, as they proudly sit up high
Little hands raise in the air, as their parents wave goodbye

The sea is getting nearer now as the sun begins to sleep

She claims a little lost shoe, its owner will probably weep
Maybe she will return it or maybe its lost for good
Maybe to return again with shells and drifting wood

The once majestic pier stands in darkness and all alone
Waves crashing up and over as she makes her final groan
More of her falls deep below and is lost forever more
Never to be seen again from Brighton's seaside shore

Jilly L Bowling

PAUL FRANKLIN

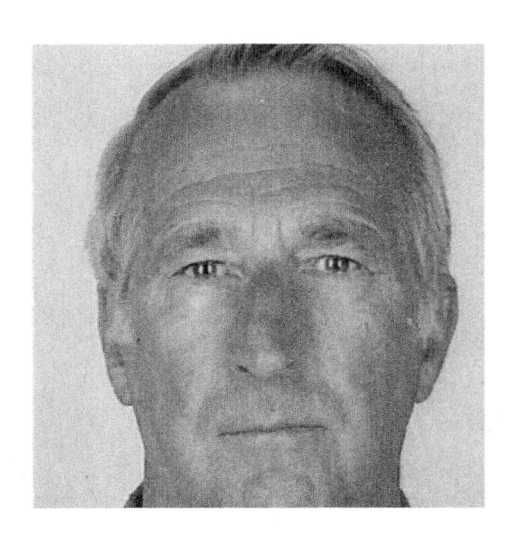

Paul Franklin was born in Cardiff in 1947. Ten years later he settled in Fareham, Hampshire when his father retired from the Royal Navy. Paul moved to Southampton when he married Sheila and now they have two grown up daughters. He spent 35 years at the Ordnance Survey, taking early retirement in 2002. Paul now lives in a cosy mobile home in Alresford.

Where we live

You live in a white thatched cottage, roses over the garden gate
I live in a grey concrete box, on a murky sink estate

You breathe country air that's fresh, with a hint of a wooden fire
All I smell is danger and despair, with a hint of a burning tyre

Farmyard animals roam your fields, cows, horses and hogs

Pit bull walkers foul my pavement, closely followed by their dogs

Your winding lanes are full of colour,
buttercup and foxglove clashing
I have coloured lights along my road, always blue and flashing

Little old shops around a village green, full of ribbons and silk
All our shops are boarded up, can't even buy a pint of milk

Just be thankful to be fit and well, live the life that's dealt you
Make the most of gifts you have, it's not
where you live but what you do

Paul Franklin

The Garden of Life

When life gets you down, you don't want to talk
No light in the tunnel, just pick up a fork

If the noise gets too loud, block out the sound
Escape from the rat race, dig in the ground

Release pent up emotion, pull up a weed
Achieve inner fulfilment, by planting a seed

As it all gets too much, this struggle and toil
When the tears start to fall, let them water the soil

If you feel useless, your mind's full of doubt
Down at your feet, new life starts to sprout

The body may feel weak, lost its will power
But it's all down to you, your seed's now a flower

Life makes you punch drunk, you just want to howl

Please take my advice, don't throw in the trowel

Paul Franklin

It's far too late

Life's not a rehearsal, you've heard it said
It's far too late when you're gone and dead

Take care of your body, you won't get another
It's far too late when you look like your mother

Remember to be pleasant, funny and kind
It's far too late when age wrecks your mind

Make a new friend each and every day
It's far too late when life's draining away

Find peace with your mate, or love that's stalled
It's far too late when your name's finally called

Cherish the day your children were born
It's far too late when the curtains are drawn

Live life to the full, whether short or long
It's far too late when they sing the last song

Don't leave this world your soul in turmoil
It's far too late when you're dust in the soil

Paul Franklin

The Cruise

When I have a holiday, I do like a long sea cruise
Lots of sun, food and sites, plus some fags and booze

I only go with the old folks, so book my trip with Saga
They don't mind if I remove my teeth, to soak in a pint of lager

I'm happy on a big cruise liner, or just a little boat
As long as it has a bar, and hopefully stays afloat

Lots to do, no time to waste, I even play the bingo
All the fours those droopy drawers, I love the sexy lingo

I like to take the fresh sea air, as I hobble along the decks
Watching all the world sail by, as I chat to the other wrecks

In sandals and shorts I wander, looking for the next sight of docks
But if it gets any damn hotter, I may take off my socks

Paul Franklin

SALLY HOLDEN

Shell

How far have you travelled tiny treasure
on your aquatic journey through the waves?
The ocean's foamy crested fingers presenting each prized piece
on to a taut sandy canvas,
the curator and creator of this organic gallery.
No one can tame the temper
of the angry white horses who
shift the shingle
and propel each delicate exhibit
for our viewing pleasure.
Rhythmic and repetitive
Rhythmic and repetitive
these aggressive watery manoeuvres,
yet our dainty porcelain survives.
framed to perfection,
seaside delectation.
A landscape portrait
tidally masterminded masterpiece.

Sally Holden

The View From Here

Uncertainty
overriding hope, for now.
But the view from here provides a constant,

if we look gently.

A limitless lushness of lawn,
each summer stem, standing tall with
fragile buds nervously dancing
towards the grand finale of bloom.

Then winter. The plants know it's coming.
Dandelions turning from a roar to a whisper.
This knowledge is our certainty, our reassurance,
Guaranteed.

Nature's creation is this predestined plan
And creativity breathes life, then movement
to my lips, to move, to smile.
Hope.

It's always here, within my view.

Sally Holden

MARK RICKENBACH

Mark has been a general practitioner and medical educator for thirty years in Chandlers Ford, near Southampton, England. His PhD looked at improving education for those in healthcare, leading to national feedback tools for medical education. He has both medical and non-medical publications including the use of song and poetry within healthcare education. His website www.docrick.co.uk gives three point tips on medical consultations, appraisal and health. Mark previously worked as an appraiser, a mentor, an Associate Dean and is currently a Visiting Professor of Healthcare at Winchester University. Having trained in East London, he worked in Portsmouth and then Australia, gaining qualifications in both secondary and primary healthcare. His three children have nearly left home and he helps coach badminton and archery in between cycling. In 2012 he was pitchside for hockey providing medical care as an Olympic gamesmaker.

One cold morning

Thick frost upon the glass
Wrinkled like older skin
The scraper cuts through
Tracks across the frozen waste

Plumes of white flakes scatter
And fall upon hands and sleeve
Inside the same
But now upon the seats and coat

Her misty face appears
Through coated glass
Approaching nearer, it seems
As melting moisture clears

Calm and ready for work
She holds a slice of toast in hand
Freshly buttered
Another melting moment

Crafted by hand that bread
Freshly baked from tin
Warm and slightly moist
A dream to savour, in the mouth

Within this car, is a treasured jewel
Sparkling with life and energy
Serene in sampling her existence
Broad smile lighting up the world

Her shoes may clutter halls
And bag upon the stairs may trip

But we treasure every moment
And shared vibrancy of her being

For she is our daughter
From giggling baby to happy toddler
Adventurous teen to loving youth
And now she's driving out to work

Mark Rickenbach
aka Dad

Blue toothpaste

Blue toothpaste on the floor
How it gets there I was never quite sure
Scattered across tiles and up to the door
Each day I return amazed to see more

A hard dry splodge, hard to remove
The guilty party a challenge to prove
Unless wet and rubbed, paste won't come away
This game every day, it seems that we play

Now it appears on the red hand towel
My favourite it is, so now I cry foul
Hard to pick off, the red it won't match
And now there's loose thread all ready to catch

This trail of blue paste leads to the source
Right near the curved tap, I ponder, of course
A well-worn and loved electric toothbrush
The culprit I now see, all used in a rush

The owner in use, spins round you see
Mind busy with work, I suspect it maybe
Or bubbling recipes, cooked up in her mind

Rushing to brush, in case she gets all behind

A lathering mouth and spinning brush head
Drips blue paste from sink to almost the bed
Her body on auto, whilst in mind it's all said
Is everyone safe, will all have been fed?

And now the blue paste has all gone
I think the owner read my song
No longer is the now perfect floor amiss
Amazed to say, this blue paste, now I really miss

Mark Rickenbach

L is for Lexi and Love

Lexi is love unconditional
All be it, biased by food
She awaits every word
Eyes fixed on me, expectant, paused

What is it now, that she wants?
Depends on the time of day
And the grumble of her tum
Look now she's barking, I wonder why?

It's eight, 8am and where's my food?
I've had it now, time to check outside
Another bark to say let me into that room
Open the curtain for my sofa top look out

And now it's time to get on that walk
Why is everyone lying around?
Get up and get going, says her urgent woof
I'm here you know, don't leave me behind

Once on the street it's busy, head down all the way
Smells a plenty to check who's been by
Friend next door or unseen foe last night?
Or even a tasty morsel, discarded in passing

Yes, Lexi is loving unconditional
With conditions attached, as suits her needs
A clockwork memory and tummy in tandem
To help us pass our time together throughout the day

Mark Rickenbach

A fortunate vaccine vex

It was Pfizer versus Oxford AstraZeneca back then
Some think they had a choice of what and when
Others had to take first come,
First serve, the decision was no sum

It seemed the choice, if given, was not so clear
mRNA from 1990s study was now here
But viral injected DNA had been around for years
Decision making, and false news, just stoked up all the fears

The short term side effects were similar, the studies say
And the long term, for both, is unknown, anyway
Pfizer more faff was frozen stored, a rush to give, once melted out
Whilst Zeneca in fridge it sat, with time to book and think about

And Pfizer was more expensive then, with Zeneca low cost
With Pfizer needing to be mixed, a sixth dose can be lost
Whilst Zeneca was ready made, eight doses to a vial
Moving it to house and home was much less of a trial

But remember how fortunate we all are
As vaccines cure and hold the exit door ajar

A miracle of science to smallpox Jenner we owe
A glimpse of light above, in tunnel dark below

The solution, I suggest, for you and me
Is much easier, as you will see
P is at middle and A or Z at ends of English Alphabet
So just go with what you are given, and accept it's what you get

Mark Rickenbach

Crisis

Chasm.
Clinging onto each opposing rock face with his finger tips.
Below. A void
Dark, long, distant, no clear end

To his right, the old life
To his left, a new life
Another life
A different life

Which way will his body swing
If he lets go of his right hand
Can he hold onto his left hand still
Can he throw his arm across and grip
Before his left hand slips

Before he falls, downward, spiralling towards nothing
Into the Unknown
An oblivion
A welcome relief
No longer clinging on
No decision to make
No longer an aching grasp to hold

To his right security and routine
To his left are the fields greener?
Is the light brighter?
The sun stronger?

Or will they fade as he crawls towards them
As he moves leftward will the right side brighten
And beckon him across the widening chasm
The right side slipped from his grasp forever

Now the right, seems right
He should have left, the left

Mark Rickenbach

Wartime England
Dogfights in the air
memories of Eileen Fisher
in 1940s Wartime England

Dogfights in the air
Spitfires, and the enemy, circle in a pair
Growling of bombers, with the sirens sound
Hendon far below, target houses on the ground

To Anderson shelter the family run
As lorry passes with anti-aircraft gun Young
girl grabs the bag and masks
"Have you the documents?" her mother asks

Dark, moist and earthy, the smell inside
Roof narrow, low and curved, floor more wide
Rickety wooden beds, candles and blankets await
The family sit down and consider their fate

The noise coming closer, to each other hold fast

Then the ground and all shakes, with one massive blast
Earth and stones rattle down on the corrugations above
Mum shouts, "It's OK my dear," as she hugs all with love

As black silence prevails, the door is now stuck
Seems they are all buried in rubble and muck Muffled
voices and shouts. "Over here, dig deep"
Relief, as they scrabble up pit walls, now so steep

Fireman father returns, shocked, to site of bomb landing
Relieved when daughter, he sees, in alleyway standing
No coupons, but butcher he gave veg and meat
And mother is cooking for all in the street!

The house is a wreck but at home they all stay
As father repairs and boards windows, working each day
The bomb it appears, from the lorry, was one of their own
Good fortune to be alive,
so no one to moan

Mark Rickenbach

BARRY RYAN

When Barry Ryan was just a year old he contracted meningitis, leaving him with cerebral palsy. He lives in Winchester with his sister and cat. In 1989 Barry had his first poem published and has had 108 poems published with Forward Press Ltd (Peterborough) and United Press Ltd (London).

Royal Hampshire County Hospital, Winchester

Thank you for being such wonderful staff,
To me - we all had a very good laugh

This is the longest in hospital since I was a kid,
Got mended, with help, I did
I am sorry to some members of staff
First it was ok, then they didn't laugh

Doctors, nurses and student
I hope you like this lovely yummy present
Thank you for showing me the hospital dynamics
From cheeky happy Barry, c six

September 28 to October 5, 2021

Barry Ryan

New achievement for The Queen

Celebrating your years, with parties and events
Ma'am, congratulations on all your achievements
That is more, than everyone from your, family tree
Now you have reached the, Sapphire Jubilee

Prince Phillip and you, were married 69 years,
Said with more, celebrating cheers
Your four children, eight grand children plus three great
Grand children, is another reason to celebrate

Thirteen Prime Ministers you had, had their say
From Sir Winston Churchill, to Theresa May
Also 13 US Presidents, you had
Eisenhower to Trump, probably some made you angry and mad

The country should make you Great, like Alfred
I am sure the public, would agree, on what I have said
I wish and happily wondered
That you still be on the throne, when you are 100

As the song goes… 'Send her victorious
Happy and glorious
Long to reign over us
God save the Queen'

Barry Ryan

TA SAUNDERS

For over 20 years TA Saunders has lived in Hampshire. With numerous poems published in anthologies and magazines, a collection of his poems is also available.

Ukraine
(I might live in Hampshire but Ukraine is always on my mind these days)

Such anger at the destruction of beautiful Ukraine
Now hell on earth
Never ending bombardment, again and again
Barbaric butchers attack
for political gain
No care or remorse
Terror bears down like driving rain
Hearts go out to everyone

in war torn Ukraine
The gruesome invaders
held in utter disdain.
Zelensky's independence fight
Great strength of character and fortitude
His relentless plight
Against this annexation, so rude.
The enemy kills hour by hour
Cut off their cash - peace will be restored
Make *them* hide and cower
Ukraine's undying strength, strikes a chord.
Good *will always* prevail
Sure as the wind doth blow
But for change, we need a gale!
The warm welcome Western glow.
When will *they* retreat?
God be with both sides
And bring about a hasty defeat.
Poor, devastated Ukraine
We watch helplessly
And feel your pain.

TA Saunders

Now

Life has suddenly got very tough
There's little laughter
More people are dying if they sleep rough
Everywhere you look, prices are higher
Food, tax, fuel and heating
Can we save cash, burning wood on the fire?
Even comedians aren't funny anymore
At the Oscars
They get punched to the floor
Meanwhile in Ukraine

There's perpetual war
My wife's fed up with me
Because in bed, I snore
How will things ever get better?
God only knows
I'll write Him a letter!

TA Saunders

Sad state of affairs

Nothing's made to last
Not like carefully made items
…of the past.
There's no quality anymore
Shelves fall apart
Knobs fall off every drawer.
Products are poorly made
Like chairs and tables
…Brand new clothes fade.
Gone is the work ethic
People haven't got what it takes
It's sad and pathetic.
Look to those we should admire
Those in power, ruling the country
Even their behaviour's dire.
…Bad parenting's to blame
For this sad state of affairs
It's such a shame.
Outsourcing parenthood
Paying others to do it
Is no good!
Children crave time with mum and dad
Not harmful gifts
- the iphone and iPad.
Children come first

Not parents' careers
A trend that must be reversed
- For Britain to become a better place
Not the worst.

TA Saunders

Education

Education can open many a door
But only if you knuckle down
Else you'll be poor.
Our time at school
Is something to cherish
…Unless you're a fool.
Each dedicated teacher
Helps us develop
Into a fine creature.
Whether private or state
Doesn't matter
A good school is great.
Your education gets you places
But you don't realise that
When you start - tying your laces.

TA Saunders

Power
(inspired by our politicians)

It goes to the head
Like a lethal cocktail
Something to dread.
Those who crave it
Can't handle it
Not one tiny bit.

Little people with big egos
Enjoy their power trips
They don't value their amigos.
Line those pockets
Feel that importance
They all need rockets.

TA Saunders

Face

Attractive or ugly?
Beauty in the eye of the beholder
A blank canvas
Young and fresh
Pockmarked and scarred
Battered and worn
Reflecting life
What lies beneath?
The face, a portrait
A unique profile
Exists for a certain time
Then vanishes without trace.

TA Saunders

TINA SHAW

At the grand age of 60, Tina Shaw graduated from Chichester University with a 2.1 degree in English and Creative Writing in 2012.

Three years earlier she had fulfilled a lifelong dream to go to university. "This was something that had been on the back burner for many years," says Tina, who lives in Stubbington.

"I still retain an interest in writing poetry some 10 years' later, although my prowess in writing short stories has somewhat lapsed these days."

Morning Sounds

Our neighbour's dog had obviously begged
For her to let him out to cock his leg.
At 4am he broke the morning silence

With a piercing bark most violent.
It shattered the peace and disturbed the birds
Who spontaneously joined in
Wishing to be heard.
Their chirps and twitters
Caused an insomniac to be more than bitter
For lack of sleep is a morning killer!

Tina Shaw

IAN WIGHT

Ian Wight is married to Jo with two children, Edward and Robert. They live in New Alresford. Ian has been writing poetry, on and off, all his life and has tended to work more in prose in recent years. He is editing a novel. In the early 1990s Ian studied Classics at Leeds University and feels that he has taken some influence (or, at least, inspiration) from both ancient and modern poets. His favourites are Catullus and Virgil of the ancients and Edward Thomas, WH Auden, Philip Larkin and Tony Harrison of the more modern. Ian's poetry tends to be driven by a regular metre and rhyme because he often finds he is sent into interesting places by the constraints of the form.

Anniversary

The cards still stand, look back at us -
strictly prim, without a fuss -

enclosed in marriage for one year.
I've watched them move, with dustings, round
their shelf, unhurried, without a sound,
and now we lay them where we'll hold them dear.
A box. Their planned-out resting place,
empty, save their forerunners' grace
in lying there, not viewed at all:
the wedding cards, in truth forgotten,
have saved a space here, at the bottom,
and there we lay them, or let them fall.
Yet I hope this won't be how it is:
years under beds with what dark gives:
a curling of edges and a fading-away.
Each year, the same, the rooting-about,
for the box from the hole, the hardly-felt clout
of cards onto cards, just another day.
With just this in mind, we've now taken in
Jo's dad's box, from his house, to begin
the gauging of life, the numbering of things,
like bank statements, photos, the cards for a birth,
love letters, pay cheques, declarations of worth
in left-behind letters, curls of hair, wedding rings.
And so now I know that the bleak box is not true,
that mementoes of past days keep them living and new.
Jo's mother and father, their love, written down,
is real in their words in a box forty years.
If our words to each other, for the other to hear,
are real still when we're not, then our love will have grown.

Ian Wight

Hampshire Autumn

The gently nodding trees, just turning gold
talk amongst themselves of change.
With practised calm, they know the old

trick of the life / unlife exchange.
Normally, this shift bothers me:
the beautifying of the world for death,
the magical way the air agrees
and makes real one's own breath.
Today, though, we have our own Spring
To brighten the air, drawn tight over sky:
our uplifting life, just made, a thing
like no other, our new perfect ally,
the comma of our baby, scanned into being
and screened to our wonder in old telly fog.
"How clear he is," the nurse says, now seeing
His head, his hands, his world tightly togged.
How aloof, I thought, a separation complete
From us, his parents, like never again.
Here he floats, Neil Armstrong, careful, discrete,
Serene in his thoughts, alone with his brain.
Later, having left him to his cherishing hush
We looked again at the pictures, single vignettes,
Yet occasioning the most overwhelming rush
Of love for him, living, the parental duet.

Ian Wight

Everyone's Life is his Passion

When Christ knew about betrayal
and He knew He'd now feel
the pains of death at the hands
of just the one who'd loved to land

delicate and heart-felt kisses,
soft and warm, on His
face, d'you think the rest
of the 'postles looked on, blessed

that they were there, or else,
thinking personally, melted
into the crowd, imagining
their own pains, burgeoning

injuries, to ham up in stories
spun out to friends and families
over years? Twelve narrators,
twelve 'I's, twelve orators.

If I'd been there, that's what
I'd have done: faded His part
down to bit player; drawn mine
out to fill the void, taken time

to make the role. Whatever
they wanted themselves, whether
gentle unassumingness or fame
they were left alone, all the same.

So we think of epitaphs before
we die, however young we are.
Did Peter think of Christ, his friend,
when faced with his own end?

No, of course not. He thought
of himself, his life, his bought
time. So it is with everyone:
play the lead, await the curtain.

Ian Wight

SHORT STORIES

fictional tales of 1,000 words and under

RAYMOND ANDERSON

Raymond Anderson lives in Bishops Waltham, Hampshire. He has been involved in Fine Art for 55 years and has been writing seriously for the past two decades.

Fortuna de la Guerra
By Raymond Anderson

"To be tactfully gross and appositely vulgar is one of the ultimate artistic refinements."
(After the Fireworks, Aldous Huxley)

Immediately on arrival in Limassol, Cyprus he was thrown into supply teaching. The subject was Biology and one that favoured textbook illustrations of cavorting bipeds as well as the quadruped variety. Children have a knack of asking provocative questions especially when already in receipt of the answers.

Our pedagogue, squirming with embarrassment, was swiftly reminded of the joys of teaching a large class of twelve year olds; the noise was frightful, it sounded like a zoo. All it needed was a few lianas dangling from the rafters; a flashy flight of cockatoos and the class would have resembled a trailer for Tarzan of the Apes.

In his dotage: he found it difficult to get tough short of a riot. Needless to say, they always stopped just short. Perhaps it was the karma he had accrued from his past.

After eighty minutes of jousting in their Punch and Judy show, he staggered out of the classroom with head ringing and his mind contemplating arsenic.

No! No! Not for the kids: it was for him. Thou shalt not grind the seed corn. Grind the seed corn? Hush. Fret not! It's the ageing chaff that gets it in the neck. We all know that animals and children can sniff out a sucker at two hundred paces. They saw him as a soft touch. He had watched other teachers flee the classroom while some had been escorted away stunned, wan, talking to themselves. It would be his turn next. Finally brought to book: committed to the care of the Cyprus Social Services. This was something else to look forward to in old age. I rather admire the dignity with which he awaits his fate.

"There can be no mistaking that somehow somewhere I came adrift," sighed Joe. "While I have never been accused of occupying the middle ground, how is it I find myself banished to the borders of popular taste? How is it that I cannot see genius in a prancing conical brassiere, Timothy Leary, Tracey Emin, Hugh Hefner, Paris Hilton, Jeff Koons, Grace Jones, Alan Carr and The Jerry Springer Show? What's up with me? Why am I so intense: so imperious: so unpretentiously obsolete? Why, when others recognise flair, do I see hype, attitude and narcissism? What do others see that I don't? When did I last see the doctor?

Perhaps lethal injection is the answer: colonic eradication. Old grumbler found twitching on carpet in death throes; progeny stood in line grasping the life insurance.

Sorry dad, but you've soiled the floor and brought the family into

disrepute. Not only are you a failed artist; you've not exactly set the world of teaching alight have you?
We've seen enough. Someone get the quicklime. No more free periods for your ilk.
You're out of date and out of time. Goodbye mister, you've had your chips!"
"Success at last," I hear you snigger, most cruel.

Man in a Denim Shirt
By Raymond Anderson

"Advertising is the rattling of a stick inside a swill bucket." (George Orwell)

With sheepish look, the man's face was seen beneath a shock of white hair. One wouldn't describe him as a beatific vision with his forehead a river of wrinkles and hands stained with iniquity. He was not, shall we say, prepossessing. However, without doubt the painter interpreted the man's craving with an assurance that illustrates the pathos of the man. Dionysus was surely the deity of this artful dodger.
While continuing to examine the semiotics of this portrait to determine whether there were any other indicators, Hugo was reminded of an incident that occurred in a hypermarket some months ago.
"Upon entering the establishment, I noticed a stack of lager cans not yards from the door; on the next shelf was a promotion of packets that bore the inscription Quick Oats. Somewhat piqued at this presumption, this worship at the shrine of youth culture; I straight away availed myself of the nearest shop assistant to enquire as to whether they stocked any Slow Oats, or perchance, Oats of a Sedate Nature. This was not done for the benefit of senior citizens with ailing reproductive powers but for those no longer able to bolt food down at the double. Whereupon, I was answered in the negative, collared and promptly shown the door.

While I made my way home I pondered as to why everything had to be done at the gallop. As I did so, requirements for Situations Vacant assailed my consciousness such as those found dominating the business columns of broadsheets. You know the sort of thing – namely, 'Should be dynamic. Preferably a slick operator. Essentially a team player. Able to work on own initiative etc.' There seemed to be a multitude of demands for employees to measure up to that stopped just short of insisting, 'Must be able to stay awake.' Then came the shampoo advertisements with their admonitions to Revive or Wash & Go! Revive? Chance would be a fine thing. Wash & Go? Whatever should we do otherwise? Wash and Dither? Rinse and Stagger? Condition and then Collapse? In the wake of this enquiry my thoughts ran riot with visions of restaurant names such as The Jovial Kitchen, The Doughty Pantry or The Happy Cheese, which looked to employ the tactic of psychological programming. Then came café names like The Hasty Tasty, The Gorge and Vanish or Scoff and Scarper, as if there was a growing tendency to eat and malinger, dine and loiter or snack and slip into a coma."

DAN BOYLAN

Dan Boylan is a retired Yorkshireman, living in Wickham, Hampshire. He has been writing articles and travel features for magazines and other publications for 25 years. "My favourite genre is short fiction, which is liberally sprinkled with intrigue and the unexpected, often with humour and a twist in the tail/tale! I create imaginative story baselines with colourful character profiles and intriguing plots," he says. Dan has been a member of various writers' groups for quarter of a century producing more than 60 short stories, dramas and rattling good yarns. "My daughter claims that I am an absolute mine of useless information," smiles Dan.

Credit Crunch
By Dan Boylan

A mobile phone bursts into life with a familiar tune.

"Hello Dad, how are you?"
"Oh, hi Polly, it always scares me when you answer like that."
"Like what?"
"Like you know who's calling before they speak."
"It's not magic Dad, your name appears in the display."
"The what?"
"On the phone, your name comes up on the phone as it rings, it's a normal feature on mobile phones. Are you OK? Haven't heard from you for a while. Everything OK at the office?"
"Well, er, no, not really, that's why I'm calling."
"Oh dear, this doesn't sound good, should I sit down?"
"Er, it's been a difficult couple of weeks and now we've just lost the Williams contract, I've had to close the assembly section and lay off several staff. The orders have dried up, I've never seen anything quite like it and it's getting worse by the day. I'm trying to hold the company together but…"
"How will it affect us, I mean the family? Will it make a change to our way of life? Or is it just a blip, something that will bounce back in a week or two?"
"Who knows what the next few weeks or months will bring? I'm having to make some serious cuts, with immediate effect, our whole finance structure is in a downturn. I've been to the bank, cap in hand, several times. I think my popularity is wearing thin. If I can put a stop on spending, I might just be able to stay afloat and avoid the company going under. I'm struggling Polly, I don't know what comes next."
"Can I help? Work a Saturday or a couple of evenings or something?"
"I'm hoping for more than that Polly."

There is a long pause.

"I've got an awful feeling that this is going to hurt. Go on Dad, let rip, out with it, what's on your mind?"
"I'm afraid you'll have to give up the flat Polly."

"The flat? My Saturday job pays for the flat and all the bills!"
"And the Mini and the allowance and I'm afraid, the college course will have to go, too."
"Blimey Dad, am I out on the street or do I have to move back into my old room and get a job at Tesco and walk to work?"
"Erm, I'm sorry Polly, your Gran has moved into your old room and I've let the granny annex to a couple who've just had their house repossessed. Things are bad Polly, everyone's having a hard time. You can have the summerhouse. I know it's a bit basic but it's all that's left. These are tough times."
"Well, things aren't going all that well here either Dad."
"Why, what's up?"
"Erm, I was going to come round on Sunday and, erm kinda, break it nice and gently."

A pause.

"Is there something I'm missing here? Has something happened that I've not been told about?"
"It's sort of difficult Dad, a bit delicate. Not the sort of thing to be discussed over the phone."
"Come on…….out with it. We're not prissy school girls. I hear all sorts of thing, every day and I'm sure that you do, too."

Another pause.

"Well, I've been seeing this guy. It's a bit complicated. He's a bit older than me but he's very sweet, very gentle……..he's"
"Older. How much older? What sort of guy? Who is he? How long has this been going on?"
"Now, Dad, calm down. Don't go getting your………"
"What were you going to tell us on Sunday, Polly? What's so secretive or fishy that you have to come home to make an announcement. What are you holding back? What's the issue here?"
"Dad, you're running away with yourself. But now that you've

worked yourself into a tizz, I'd best tell you what it's all about. You see, erm, well, erm, you might be a Granddad by next summer. There, I've said it. It's out in the open."

"What? You're pregnant and to an older man? Oh Polly! Your Mum will go crazy, you know what plans she's always had for a big wedding for you. What sort of guy is this?"

"Well, he's married with kids but they're about to split up......"

"Oh my God......."

"And I know it sounds bad but he's waiting to go to court...."

"Oh Polly........"

"He borrowed his mate's car but it was nicked and the coppers stopped him on the M27....."

"Oh it just gets worse......."

"He's got a suspended sentence and he might go to jail....."

"This is just wonderful. Your mum will freak out."

"We can't get a bigger flat 'cause he's got a bad credit rating and his credit cards have been cancelled."

"Anything else? Should I brace myself or is there any good news?"

"I wondered if you could lend us five grand until he gets back on his feet. We'll pay you back after we get back from the Caribbean."

"Caribbean?"

"Oh, we thought we would have a couple of weeks in the Caribbean if we could get the dosh. Do you feel generous?"

"Oh Polly, what have you done? Are you going to throw away all the hard work you've done in your education to go with this clown, this loser?"

"But I love him Dad, I just want to be with him all the time. Please try to understand and be nice to him. And try not to make it sound so bad for Mum."

A pause.

"I just can't get my head around all this. Yesterday, you were a happy go lucky teenage student, today you're skirting at the edge of disaster, prepared to throw everything away on some whim, I just don't see......"

"I know Dad and it wouldn't be so bad if things at the company and things at home weren't in such a bad state."
"The company? Oh, I made all that up for a wind-up. The company's as strong as ever, I was just having a laugh with you……"
"I know, I was speaking with Julie the receptionist yesterday and she told me she was fed up with all the overtime and new orders coming in. I spoke to Gran too and she told me that she's having the annex redecorated."
"Well, you little vixen………"
"And there is no married boyfriend, pregnancy or anything else………I just made all that up to show you that you're not the only one who can tell whoppers and do wind-ups."
"Oh, it's all a bit of a pity really, I was rather getting to like the idea of being a Granddad by next summer!"

Cost of loving
By Dan Boylan

It was just after 6pm on a wintery, Saturday evening in the pub.

Tracey "All right, Shirley?"
Shirley "Yeah, Jeff's coming in later, been playing football with Nigel."
Tracey "Oh, right."
Shirley "Just seen your Dad in the snug Trace, watching the telly."
Tracey "Yeah, it's the Chelsea game, not going to miss the Chelsea game, is he?"
Shirley "Your Mum comin' in later?"
Tracey "Nah, she's in Tenerife."
Shirley "What, without your Dad?
Tracey "He don't like the heat, nor the food with all that olive oil an' garlic and he's happier at home watching telly.
Shirley "Oh, who's she gone with then, your Mum, her bingo mates?"

Tracey (lowering her voice) "Naw, she's gone with her fancy man!"
Shirley "Fancy man? Your Mum's got a fancy man?"
Tracey "Yeah, it ain't nothin' special. Dad don't like the heat an' that, don't care for dancin' or foreign food, so he stays here with all his home comforts and Mum goes off to Spain to live it up for a while."

A pause.

Shirley "Does he know, I mean does your Dad know erm, what's going on?"
Tracey "Naw, he thinks she's gone with a bunch of the girls from work. It's end of January, you know forth round of the FA cup and all that; she buys him a couple of crates of Watney's, fills the freezer with pies and ready cooked meals and he spends all week watching football. Put him in front of the telly with footie, a plateful of pie an' mash and a bottle or two and he's as happy as a sand-boy! So, Mum goes off to Tenerife and bosch, everyone's happy. You ready for another?"

Another pause.

Tracey "Look, it ain't no big deal Shirl, it's different strokes for different folks, me Dad's a bit of a stick in the mud, me Mum still thinks she's a teenager. He's happy in his slippers in front of the box, Mum love's dressing up, fine food and wine and dancing the night away. She's the life and soul of the party, my Mum, while me Dad's got one foot in the grave! If you know what I mean."
Shirley "But don't he know?"
Tracey "No he don't and what he don't know won't hurt him. What's the point in trying to make him or her change their ways, at their age? She's got no interest in football, he's got no interest in dancing. They just have a week or so doing their own thing, two or three times a year."
Shirley "Two or three times a year?" Shirley exploded.
Tracey "All right, all right Shirl, keep yer voice down, we don't

want this getting into the Sunday papers! It ain't no big deal but it is my business, our business now, so keep yer trap shut," snapped Tracey and she rose, took their empty glasses and headed for the bar.

When she returned, Shirley still wore a pained expression.

Shirley "Don't he ever ask her how she got on? Or what she did or where she went?"
Tracey "No he don't and she don't ask him who won the bleedin' football. Look Shirl, Mum an' Dad went on holiday to Spain about ten years ago, he had too many St Miguels one lunchtime and fell asleep on the beach without his shirt on, got sunburnt and spent the rest of the holiday indoors. Next year he insisted on a week in Southend. It poured all week so they sat in the pub watching telly. Next year she went to Spain with her sister and he stayed at home, sorted, an' everybody was happy!"
Shirley "Does you mum and erm whats-his-name, erm, do they, well, you know............?"
Tracey "God's sake Shirley, grow up! Do you think they had separate bedrooms? Fancy man don't mean just good friends, it means lover, mistress, a bit on the side. It means dirty weekends, sexy nighties, naughty an' nice and nudge-nudge, wink-wink!"
Shirley "Well, you don't wrap it up in cotton wool, do you Trace? You lay it all out, warts an' all, don't you. I can't pretend I'm not shaken, not least with your, your attitude to it all." Tracey shrugged, indifferently.
Shirley "Who does she tell your Dad she's going away with?"
Tracey "Told you, girls from work."
Shirley "And what about him, what about the fancy man?"
Tracey "I dunno, tells his missus he's playing golf with his mates, I think!"
Shirley "Where's the fancy man come into it then? Who is he then?"
Tracey "She's known him for years. They were in the same class at school or something. Later, they worked in the same office at

Gibson's, used to sit with each other in the canteen, then they went on a weekend course together, it sort of snowballed from there." Tracey said simply.
Shirley "Oh my God!"
Tracey "Listen Shirl, there's nothing wrong with it. Nobody's stealing anything, nobody knows, so nobody gets hurt. It's like we shared a flat. You go on holiday so I borrow your bike all week. When you come back your bike is just where you left it. No harm done, don't cost you anything and I save a week's bus fares," she grinned and winked.
Shirley frowned and grimaced as she took it all in. Scratching her head, then her cheek, she tried to make sense of it all. Suddenly, her face brightened.
Shirley "It'll be the end of the football season in April, what'll your Mum do then, Trace?"
Tracey "Nice thinking Shirley but me old Mum is a couple of strides ahead of you. Dad enjoys cricket as well as football, so Mum's just bought him a season ticket for all the matches at the Ageas Bowl! She says that it's money well spent............ she calls it SportsAid."

Seize the day!
By Dan Boylan

The train rattled north through the darkened towns and countryside, emitting the occasional blast from its steam whistle. Soldiers littered the narrow corridor, their kit-bags, rifles and greatcoats, strewn carelessly along its length. They'd let the civilians have the compartments and they strolled aimlessly back and forth, smoking and laughing. A family of seven occupied the last compartment, eastern Europeans, perhaps, poorly dressed, edgy, frightened, darting eyes, their life's possessions stuffed into a series of battered suitcases, now piled high on the luggage rack. No one cast them a second glance, the war had brought wave upon wave of such refugees into the country.
The boy took ill somewhere north of Peterborough. He uttered

a long groan, clutched his stomach and slid silently to the floor of the compartment. The family gathered around him, pleading, panicking, jabbering in their alien tongue. They watched in horror, in the dimly lit carriage as his eyes closed, he shook violently and he slipped into unconsciousness.

Twenty minutes later, at Grantham, Papa leaped out onto the blacked-out platform, deeply covered in uniforms and kit-bags, waving his arms wildly. He grabbed a passing porter and begged, "Please, you help? My boy, he is sick!"

The station master soon appeared and climbed into the carriage. He walked unhurriedly forward, glanced at the lad then felt his forehead. He called the porter through the open window, "Ambulance, Harry! And sharpish!"

"No, no sir," pleaded Papa in a panic. "We go Glasgow. We meet boat for New York. All family."

"You can go with the boy to the hospital, sir," the station master said soothingly.

"No, no." He persisted, "Boat. She leave at six o'clock," and he turned to his eldest girl and snapped a question at her. She replied in English, "Tomorrow. The word is tomorrow!"

"Ja, ja, tomorrow. We meet boat tomorrow. Is last boat, all family go New York. We no wait!"

"The lad goes to hospital, or he dies. One of you must stay with him," The station master ordered.

The girl, in her late teens, was dark and calm. She translated this and the family broke into a near panic. Mama threw back her head, wailing. Papa fell to one knee and pleaded. The youngsters clung to each other, whimpering and weeping.

Suddenly, the peel of a bell grew louder heralding the imminent arrival of the ambulance. The station master, anxious for the train to depart on time, said firmly, "One of you must stay with the boy." This brought only another bout of cries and anguish.

"I will stay Papa!" announced the stern-faced girl. Another wail of anguish echoed across the station platform. She spoke softly then to her father; she pointed to the train, then to the family and to the arrival of the ambulance men with their stretcher. Papa wept and put his hands to his mouth. The girl stroked his back and soothed him. Then she turned, hugged Mama, then ushered them back onto the train, kissing them all. "Katerina, Katerina," they wailed. Papa leaned out of the window and thrust a handful of bank notes at her. She smiled, turned to the station master and nodded. He touched his cap thankfully, blew his whistle and waved his flag and the train began to move slowly forward. Seconds later, all that remained was a silence and the lingering whiff of smoke in the cold and dark night air.

She sat quietly in the back of the ambulance, holding her brother's hand. It had been a long journey across the plains of central Europe, the beginning of an epic migration that would eventually take them to uncle Milo's small farm, deep in the plains of Idaho. It was arranged that the family would live in a small cabin on the edge of the farm and grow potatoes. The girl would stay at home and help Mama with the children and the chores, in keeping with the family tradition. When the youngest child left home, then perhaps if she could find a man, she would be free to marry.

Now, for her, there would be no farm in Idaho. She would stay in England. She would find a job, a room and maybe train to be a nurse. She bent towards her brother, stroked his face and whispered, "Bravo tovarich. Bravo. That was a superb performance. Charlie Chaplin couldn't have played the part any better!"

JUDITH DAVEY

Judith Davey was born in Lyndhurst, Hampshire. She is a proud mum, Methodist and a curious person, who loves to know about the world (she has qualifications in subjects including dog behaviour). She loves to dance the Argentinian Tango (and has danced in Barcelona, Berlin, Malmo and Porto). Judith lives with her husband, Adrian in a brick and flint thatched cottage in Abbotts Ann, in the beautiful Test Valley. Passionate about social justice, Judith works in a charity specialising in health and social care.

Why I loved my son's funeral
By Judith Davey

My son Ben's remains are buried under the sunflowers beside a large oak tree. The sheep in the field munch the flowers. In the late afternoon we celebrate his life so that we can see the beautiful sunset. The tent is illuminated with lights and candles that twinkle as the dark arrives.

I love his funeral. And Ben would love it, too.

Even in rude health, my family talk about death and what our last wishes are. Ben had picked the spot ten years before; the humanist burial meadow just outside Bath. We also knew what music he wanted. Some of the same pieces that were played at my mum's funeral (which will also be played at mine).

There are so many characters at the celebration of his life. From toddlers to the elderly. And quite a number of dogs, too. One of Ben's friends wears a dressing gown; he's a patient in a local mental health hospital and has just come out for the funeral. Does he have permission?

Another of his friends wears a tailcoat, waistcoat, bow tie and top hat as a mark of respect for Ben. He is slightly worse for wear and seems to be leaning at a 45 degree angle.

Quite a number of mourners share memories or funny stories. Ben's brother Tom's story is poignant and full of love. Some just sob. I put my arm around one of Ben's friends, who is crying as the celebrant speaks. I smile because Ben would have done the same thing. Everyone has the opportunity to scatter some of his ashes and some take his ashes home with them. We give everyone packets of wildflower seeds with "in memory of Ben" written on them, to plant afterwards. God is with us in that meadow even though it is a humanist celebration.

The celebration of Ben's life is such a contrast to the circumstances of his death. We don't know exactly when he died and his lifeless body had not been treated with respect or dignity when he was found. My last memory of him was that his face was green and purple with decomposition.

Do I feel angry that my son died? Someone who would always cross the road to help others without question or reward and who would always help even if it was not in his own interests? You bet. But I know that my son's life and death has inspired others. So what is irrecoverable for me is helping others. My son was such a good example of so many things that it gives me comfort to know that he lit the rugged path for others. He helped others carry their own crosses. Something I've not seen often in my life.

I now know that God is crying with me at what happened to my boy. It was the warmth and grace of local faith communities that made the difference; their faith helped me rediscover mine.

Blessings are funny things. Sometimes they're obvious, palpable, tangible. But sometimes they're harder to spot. Sometimes blessings are hard won or come out of the most desperate situations. Like diamonds or coal, both are formed under extreme pressure and both are valuable in their different ways.

I now realise that you have to acknowledge your pain and loss. Embrace it but do not allow yourself to be consumed by it. Who'd have thought that blessings could come out of Ben's ashes?

My prayer is that when you are experiencing loss and grief, that you too feel God's arms around you because he is crying with you.

SUSAN GREY

Susan lives in Chandler's Ford. Even though she was brought up in a city in Hampshire she enjoys the countryside and the sea. "I've always used writing as a therapy and inspiration."

Circle of Time
by Susan Grey

Inspiration for this particular story came from a conversation while travelling on board a cruise liner with her husband, who was working as an officer at the time.

It was on a soggy miserable Sunday in November, Alan crunched along the gravel driveway and at last reached his parent's home. Letting himself in, the first thing he noticed was the deep pile cream carpet, the highly polished mahogany hall table and the scarlet wallpaper.

He was genuinely surprised – Mum and Dad had really gone to town spending on the house while he had been working away at sea for several months. Exhausted from his transatlantic voyage, he needed to collapse into the nearest available chair and enjoy the delights of an English cup of tea. Nowhere in the world came close to this, not even on board the luxury cruise liner he'd left that morning. Through weary eyes he observed the living room was where they had really splashed out. Another plush new carpet and a very inviting chocolate brown Draylon sofa with two oversized matching chairs. Perhaps they had won the Pools and not told him; although he was slightly disgruntled they didn't have one single ashtray in the house.

Despite his exhaustion, the aroma of home baking proved an irresistible magnet and summoned him to the kitchen. Apart from the tangerine pendant light dominating the centre of the ceiling and the floral dishes neatly stacked next to the cooker, the kitchen was virtually the same. He helped himself to two fresh cream and strawberry jam scones and switched the kettle on.

Jean Archer was totally unprepared for the faint smell of cigarette smoke, which greeted her when she entered the house about 20 minutes later. She immediately collided with the oversized scuffed tan suitcase casually abandoned in the middle of the hall.

"Oh, that's another pair of tights gone, what on earth.........."

The sight she witnessed in the living room rendered her temporarily speechless; she gasped a sharp intake of breath.

Alan was sprawled half asleep; in his crumpled travel clothes, lying across her brand new sofa; his tired pungent smelling shoes scattered across the floor. A lit cigarette was becoming shorter as it perched precariously on the edge of the pristine white saucer, which had dribbled tea in its recess.

"Who the hell are you?" Jean's booming voice made him shoot up in startled amazement, like an animal cornered in the glare of car headlights; the bone china tea cup and saucer now landed head first on the pale green Axminster.

"What the ....?" His sleepy eyes narrowed. "Hey," he smiled

nervously. "You're not my Mum."

"Well that's an accurate observation." Jean folded her arms defiantly nodding.

"I most certainly am not," she spat the words out, her face like thunder and tossed his legs to one side, his bare feet landed heavily on the soft deep piled carpet. The remnants of a fruit scone floated to the floor like a fine spray of confetti. A small dollop of strawberry jam stuck tenaciously to his chin.

It was at this precise moment I came wandering into the living room, scantily clad in a white towelling dressing gown blissfully unaware that much earlier, while I enjoyed a delicious rose scented bubble bath engrossed in my music, a total stranger was wandering about downstairs.

"Julie, you get dressed," Mum ordered.

Of course my Mum's bark was worse than her bite and she was prepared to patiently listen about the post going astray and Alan's parents moving to Wales. Their letter never reached him. Alan still had the old key. After he enjoyed a proper cup of tea, good home cooking and overnight stay, he trekked off again in search of his new home. I'm glad to say we exchanged contact details because today in this age of high speed, progressive global technology, time has gone full circle.

Alan and I have just celebrated a landmark anniversary. Mum wouldn't recognise the infrastructure now. The area boasts easy access to the international airport, with plans for a new high speed railway link. Our house and entire street have long gone to make way for the prestigious shopping centre, state of the art cinema complex and two hotels.

MAX HARRIS

Max Harris was born and educated in Oxford. He enjoyed a range of occupations including work as a sub-editor but needed to explore his entrepreneurial yearnings and moved into the construction and restoration world. He has enjoyed many challenges together with a busy family life. Retirement was enforced early because of a life-changing road traffic accident but allowed him to enjoy several years of Iberian sunshine. He now enjoys a slower lifestyle shared between Bishop's Waltham, Hampshire and Devon, writing short stories, composing crossword puzzles and making model boats of Nelson's era.

An infinitesimal slice of endless time
By Max Harris

My body creaks, I am viewed as vulnerable, so another day to sit and ponder, another time to reflect on my past.
It all started in University Parks, Oxford in 1957. High summer. Her school visited the city for the day to look at the architecture of the colleges. We met, laid in the grass, frolicked and kissed. The kiss moved like a warm light from the centre of my heart. But she had to return to the coach to go back to Bournemouth, back home. She was a real head turner.
We stayed in touch by phone and letters but my hologram of her drifts into the dark fog of night. Finally she agreed to spend the night with me. Urgently we met in Brighton because I thought she might go to Australia.
Early on a sunny Saturday afternoon we met again, I didn't take

her any flowers. We started to search for a bed and breakfast but many of them were full and perhaps others weren't happy with two young teenagers seeking a room.

The night was beginning to take a serious hold and we were getting desperate but finally a woman reluctantly rented us a room. It smelt of Lemon Pledge and had Anaglypta wallpaper, small, tidy but not fit for my queen. Strange isn't it, remembering the room but not recalling her name? Leaves me desolated.

Rapidly we slid under the covers. I could feel her heart, hear her breathing. I loved her skin and we held each other close.

At the station we kissed goodbye. "Enjoy Australia," I said. With her school friend she had applied for a visa. In those days you could emigrate for £10.

Now I wish I could find her and say how sorry I am for the way I treated her. Did she stay or did she go? What happened to her? Remorse is hurtful. Memories sometimes are sweet, aren't they?

JENNIFER MCDERMOTT

Jennifer lives in the village of Abbotts Ann with her husband and three young children: Amelia, Alexandra and Sebastian. She is a corporate solicitor and enjoys writing, yoga and pilates. This is her first short story.

Trevelyan
by Jennifer McDermott

Trevelyan. Their forever home. The house stood at the end of a private road. Red brick, with a neat front lawn and a pretty rose garden along the side of the wide driveway, leading to the large family garden. Resplendent with a swing swaying from the expansive apple tree. Homemade from a beautifully smooth piece of wood and slightly frayed ropes for the children's chubby hands to clasp.

A happy family home. Two beautiful children. A dark-haired, blue-eyed girl and a mischievous blond baby boy with twinkling brown eyes. At first, Martha ignored those goose bumps when they came. That feeling of being watched. She was being silly. The home was perfect, she told herself. Nothing to worry about. At least it had been, it seemed to her, until her baby boy arrived. He was such a happy child; placid and calm. With an infectious smile, despite his flushed cheeks as those first new teeth began to cut through. She had been too tired and all consumed by their new arrival to notice at first. Yet, she had become increasingly aware of a sense of unease in the back bedroom where her son's cot stood. Her daughter had rejected the larger bedroom in favour of a smaller, cosier bedroom at the end of the generous landing. Already wiser than her years.

Martha hadn't mentioned it to her husband. He wouldn't entertain her fears, given his staunch Catholic upbringing. No need to trouble him when he was working so hard to keep up with the mortgage payments. In the end, she hadn't needed to mention it. It became more palpable - the coldness in that room.

That day she simply couldn't settle her usually content baby boy, despite her very best efforts. Martha tried to convince herself that his front teeth were coming through. Yet, she could feel it; an icy cold presence immediately behind her that evening as she lay him in the cot. His screaming started up again before she had even closed the door behind her.

Martha's complexion was unusually pale. It was enough of a hint for her husband to take up the mantle. In fact, he was very willing to sneak in some cuddles with his boy after a busy day in the office. Barely two minutes had passed when he abruptly returned to their bedroom with their son.

"He's not sleeping in there tonight," Edward insisted in a low voice.

She knew he felt it, too. Exhausted, the young mother didn't raise the subject at that moment. She happily allowed her husband to nestle their son in between them in their bed and the three allowed sleep to silently wash over them. Like a warm, comforting bath, pulling them beneath its surface.

The next day, as she gazed out of the car window, her mind toyed with what had happened the night before. Edward was driving and, without warning, suddenly muttered, "There was something there in that room last night." A statement rather than a question. "Did you feel it?"

His question was enough to raise goosebumps on her arm, even though the car was warm and the day fine and sunny. In an instant, she was transported back. Relief coursed through her body. She wasn't going mad. Martha had noticed it weeks ago. The coldness. That feeling of being watched. It was getting worse. Almost as if they weren't welcome in their own home. Pictures falling from the wall without explanation. The radio playing in the night. They had put that incident down to old wiring. Yet she knew that electrical issues hadn't caused the lightbulb to shoot from its socket in her daughter's bedroom. Surely that was impossible, wasn't it? The family cat would say otherwise. He had leapt out of his skin moments before. Some sort of sixth sense at play?

Martha hadn't wanted to consider any alternative explanation. Not after they had plunged their savings into this beautiful house. Yet curiosity niggled in her bones. Almost impossible to ignore. That inquisitive nature of hers had made her raise it, in casual conversation, with her neighbour, Sally. Innocently trying to direct the conversation to see if Sally had any inkling about the history of the house next door. Sally's face seemed to cloud over for a fleeting moment and then her sunny smile reappeared. She had not lived there long enough to know any history about the houses in Oak Lane.

Martha's questions surfaced again the next day at the local library. She loved taking the children there. Her daughter's face full of innocent excitement; delighted to explore the myriad of books on offer. The archive section beckoned Martha. No harm in taking a quick look on a computer as her son dozed contentedly in his pushchair and her daughter curled up in a cosy low chair with a new picture book.

At first nothing of note. Until something most certainly did catch her eye. The headline caused a sharp intake of breath. The colour drained from her cheeks. Like her world had suddenly jolted. There in black and white; "Trevelyan Tragedy". The photo underneath was what had truly caused her to gasp. For it could have been them, a woman, and her blond boy, smiling at the camera. The boy was very similar in colouring to her son, although clearly slightly older. She read the article. The mother had not seen the car. A tragic accident. The little boy had darted into the road and been knocked over by a car, driven by a young local lad. Despite the very best efforts of those at the scene, the child had died. Not on the road but in the house itself. Her house. Now someone, or something, from that forgotten family lingered on, in the house; trapped in torment and agitated by the promise of new life blossoming in her boy's bedroom.

VICKI MORRIS

Growing up in Chilbolton, near Stockbridge in rural Hampshire, Vicki Morris has a passion for thrillers with a twist. With a full-time career in the audio and marketing industry and as a mum of two grown up children, she likes to use her spare time and imagination to create a little mystery and romance. Spending time in her allotment garden gives Vicki, who now lives in Picket Piece, just outside Andover, quiet inspiration to write short stories and novels.

All Good Causes
by Vicki Morris

How did this always happen? How was she always caught up in these seemingly random, crazy situations? Margot had never found it easy to say no or question the decision of those around her for fear of standing out or getting noticed, but this time even she knew it would have been the safer option. Margot didn't have strong opinions on much. Generally she just tried to go with the flow, but the welfare of innocent animals seemed like (if one were going to have a cause) something she should care about. But out here, in the dark, surrounded by strangers she was beginning to doubt that this was anything to do with cute little bunnies. Her expectations of maybe holding a plaque, shouting with the crowd, and then going to the pub for a few to celebrate the good deed had completely diminished.

Simon was passionate about his cause, well, all causes in fact. If it meant he could break in somewhere, cause trouble, damage other people's property he was getting his thrills. The fact that others wanted to join him and celebrate his actions, all in the name of the cause, made it perfectly legitimate in his eyes. He was equally excited this evening as he'd got the nerdy sheep Margot to join him and his co-conspirators. She was of course an easy target because she wouldn't say no to him. He knew that she really liked him. She'd given in to his advances easily enough to prove that, but he didn't care. He still got a thrill from enticing her and knowing when trouble came, and it would, that she would be the one left standing, taking the fall for him.

Margot couldn't deny she got such a thrill when she was with Simon. He was the ultimate bad boy. Throwing caution to the wind, two fingers to the establishment, doing everything that in her eyes any 17-year-old wanted to but was too afraid to do. He was rebellious and as a result had been requested to leave the college that they both attended. That hadn't stopped him hanging around though and Margot knew she had been swept away by the attention he gave her. Not that he was particularly nice to her, embarrassing her and generally making her feel she was inadequate, but at least he noticed. It was more than she believed anyone else did for her so she'd take it and hope that one day he would realise she was the one for him and they could be rebels together.

So, this Tuesday evening having drunk vodka from the bottle, smoked a cigarette for the first (and last) time Margot was here, helping Simon and his crew, Tash, Pete, and newcomer to the group Greg, climb into an animal rescue centre. This wasn't just any rescue centre. Simon had assured them that the animals weren't re-homed but in fact destroyed to get them off the streets. They were going to free them from the terrible fate that was sure to await them. She knew that if she was caught it would be devastating for her parents and she would have to explain everything but right now that felt like the point. She was doing what she wanted, not what someone else was telling her to do.

Within just a matter of minutes here they all were, within the centre, surrounded by cages. Margot stood near a feeding station, which was positioned at the end of the corridor. Cages either side containing a whole variety of dog breeds. She thought about how sad they looked, some were startled by the sudden arrival of their rescuers, others started to bark loudly, angry and aggressive. At the far end of the room with its dusty floors and metal roof, was a room with a sign saying 'vet' on the door. Simon was heading straight for it, forcing his way to the front of the group to get there first. Was this where the poor creatures met their fate? Margot pushed to follow Simon. She wanted to share his joy at bringing this barbaric institution to a close. She got close but he pushed her back, almost violently. Looking out for her even in the height of the situation, not wanting her in danger, proving that he cared for her, she thought.

The next few minutes happened in slow motion and yet felt so fast. Margot felt an arm wrap round her waist and pull her back, away from Simon. She struggled, lashed out wanting to be free but whoever had her was too strong, too persistent. There were suddenly a lot more people in the room, people in uniforms, shouting. The dogs were getting hysterical adding to the frenzy. The cold air hit her and along with bright car headlights reawakened Margot's senses. She had been dragged outside and now the reality of the situation started to dawn.

Getting in with the group had been easy for Greg, he'd known of Simon from his half sister and Simon's previous tag along girlfriend. Greg could play up to Simon, pretend to be impressed by him, gain his trust. That's how he'd known of the plan to break into the rescue centre to steal the veterinary drugs, to impress, to use and of course sell. It would have been easy just to let the authorities know and let it run its course but there was Margot. He couldn't let anything happen to her. She of course had no idea how he felt, she had been entranced by Simon and no talking was going to change her mind. He had to rescue her, let her see what Simon was, and then he prayed she would want him as much as he wanted her. She would fall in love with him.

LORRAINE MURRAY

Lorraine Murray is originally from Dublin and now lives in a small village in Hampshire. She works full-time for the NHS and writes from time to time. Her writing, to this point, has been mainly on her blog, which focused on minimalism and the freedom it can bring. Reading and theatre are her two main interests, along with doting on her 14-year-old cat.

The Stranger
By Lorraine Murray

It was a dark and stormy night. We were on our way back from my grandmother's house when the car broke down. Again. The third time that month. The first time meant we were late to bed and for us kids that was excitement. The second time was boring while we waited for a tow. The third time was a bit frightening. My mother was driving, my younger brother was silent, my little brother was crying, and my father was dying of cancer.

My first self-important thought was that my role as big sister was clearly to be the sustaining and nurturing figure as my mother tried to figure out what to do and my father sat, angry and helpless. But my little brother pushed me away, crying too hard to make himself understood. Willing the car to get going, I promised her a rest if she just got us home. Previously, my silent conversations with the car seemed to work. I pushed away thoughts of tow trucks and jump leads. But this time, no matter how hard I tried, she wouldn't co-operate.

Today's world, with our mobile phones and our constant communications capability. Do you know what it's like to be alone in the dark, with no thought of rescue, no contact, no connection? Mum asked Dad tentatively, "How long would it take me to run back to your mother's house?"

"Out of the question," he growled.

"Did we pass a phone box? Or I wonder if we could …."

Suddenly our car was flooded with light. I heard a car door slam and footsteps slowly approach. I could feel my father tense up, even though he was sitting diagonally across from me.

"Hello there."

My mother's hand crept to the door handle then hesitantly moved upwards to the window winder. Slowly, she wound the window down a little.

"Having car trouble?"

"Yes, it's the …"

"No, we're fine," my father cut in firmly.

I could see the man's eyes pass from my mother in the driving seat, to my father in the passenger seat, to us three kids in the back. This was the 1970s – this wasn't the usual configuration of a family in a car.

"Give the engine another turn."

My mother turned the key, let out the choke and pressed the accelerator.

"Now, now," I silently begged the spluttering car. "You've done it before, start now."

Nothing.

"Yes, I see, nothing happening there. Where do you live?"

My father glared. I could feel my mother's mind waft over her three children in the back, as lightly as a kitten's breath.

"Hazelwood."

He whistled. "Hazelwood – that's a good bit away. What brings you all the way out here, then?"

"Visiting my mother," answered my father. "And all my brothers," he added, in a warning tone.

"Well, you'll have to leave it for tonight. You won't get anyone out on a Sunday. And no-one will steal it," he said, looking at our car disparagingly.

"I know, I know, but how are we ever to get home?" My mother was on the verge of tears.

I might have been young but even I knew there was no money for the extravagance of a taxi, let alone money to have the car properly repaired.

"Hop in, I'll take you," said the man cheerfully.

"What?" My mother wasn't sure she had heard correctly.

"How else will you get home?" The man's glance fell on the frail form of my father, the walking stick resting across his knee and the frightened faces of three children.

"We're not getting into a car with a stranger, and that's final," said my father.

At the same time, my mother said, "God will reward you for this."

In a minute, we were in a strange car, with a strange man. I sat in the back with my brother on my lap and my younger brother on my mother's lap. The man had gently helped my father into the front of the car and placed his walking stick in his hand.

The journey was uneventful. Instead of grumbling at how many red lights we encountered, they seemed to all be green. Instead of pointing out the landmarks that made the journey usually seem shorter, "look, that's the hospital that you were born in," "look, that's the house that looks like a castle," we were silent, with my father murmuring directions as we got nearer home.

When we arrived my little brother was asleep. I was vaguely aware of my father trying to press money into the stranger's hand and it being waved away, of my mother promising to pray for him and assuring that God would not forget him.

That night I remember falling into bed and sleeping such a deep sleep.

Within six months my father was dead. In the aftermath, we experienced such kindness and thoughtfulness from family and friends.

I have often thought of that stranger. Can you imagine, coming across a family of three children, a worried woman, a sick man and walking towards them, not walking away? Of driving across a city? Of doing such a kindness, without wanting anything in return.

I have thought of that man many times in my life. I could have passed him in the street and not known him. I never even knew his name.

TA SAUNDERS

For over 20 years TA Saunders has lived in Hampshire. He was business and motoring editor of the Bournemouth Echo. A prolific writer, he regularly contributes to publications in England and America.

The following story is in memory of Neal Butterworth, editor of the Bournemouth Echo (1998 to 2011), who spearheaded many successful fundraising campaigns. A talented sportsman, Neal was selected to play football for Manchester City but chose to pursue a career in journalism instead. He still found time to play football and cricket though. Neal was an inspiring and greatly respected, kind hearted, family man. In 2007, alongside actor Martin Clunes, he received an honorary doctorate from Bournemouth University. Six years later Neal died from cancer, aged 55.

Newspaper man

By TA Saunders

"We need more sales, Jim," urged the regional director in his harsh Yorkshire accent. "I've got head office breathing down me neck and if we don't pull a rabbit out of the hat it won't just be me that's out of a job."

In the six months that Jim Delaney had been editor of the local paper, readers had left, advertising revenues had dropped and newspaper sales had slumped.

"It's not a reflection on you Jim, the paper's lost its way, which is why you were hired in the first place. We must get it back to the heart of the community. Let's have a meeting tomorrow at 8am in the board room. Bring your ideas."

Meetings were the bane of Jim's life; this, the tenth of the week and it was only Tuesday. As editor his principal interest was in writing not liaising with the circulation and advertising departments about commercial aspects. He appreciated that this was necessary but it didn't interest him in the way that writing his daily column did. He was directly responsible for a team of journalists and between them they compiled the daily newspaper and a plethora of specialist publications. The bottom line was profit. A pressurising job.

Cycling to and from work gave him the time to think. In fact it was often while on the saddle that he thought of his best ideas. That night he went home utterly exhausted, mentally and physically. He wasn't given to panic or worry but even he had to admit it was looking a bit dicey when, as he set off for work at 430 the following morning, he still had no ideas for saving the paper. Riding along on the empty road in the dark, the wind blowing on his face his head became clearer and he felt more focussed.

Later on in the board room

"So what have you got for me then?" quizzed his boss, Derek Smithson.

"Like you say, this paper needs to be at the heart of the

community."

"Yes."

"Therefore, we need to actually support the community, not just churn out the same old puff."

"I'm listening," replied Derek. "What do you have in mind?"

"We need to get behind good causes. We need to be on their side, understand them better than we do."

"That's bold," Derek looked thoughtful, weighing up the pros and cons.

"And off the back of it not only will we be seen to be actually promoting important local issues, we'll be able to generate more news. You know, human interest stories."

"It's a risk but we're on our knees. I've already had to lay off half the workforce. Alright, you've got six months to turn round this sinking ship."

On the way back to his office Jim considered what local causes he could get behind. It needed to be more than that though. His desk was littered with press releases. His inbox was full of them, too. Most would be binned. One stood out above all the rest. 'Take part in Triathlon South this spring'. His attention pricked, he read on. A keen sportsman he had had trials for a premiership football team and been accepted but had declined the offer in favour of journalism. Now in his mid 30s he could still run fast and swim while cycling was his passion. But did he have the stamina to complete a 10km route? Undaunted he shouted out to his secretary, "Lozza."

"Yes, sweetheart," came the reply, from his ageing secretary, who pretended to be younger.

"Can you sign me up for this?" he took the form through to Lorraine. "We need to get busy. I need a charity to support and I need sponsorship. This'll make a good picture story for tomorrow's rag. Get a snapper to meet me in the garage pronto."

She stood up, clicked her heels and saluted him, enjoying seeing his newfound enthusiasm.

Shutting the door he threw off his suit and clambered back into his cycling outfit. He ran down to the garage to find his bike. "Jez," he said, catching one of the photographers having a sly cigarette. "Take a few pics of me with the bike."

This was exciting, he was savouring this burst of adrenalin. The staff would be sure to sponsor him and he would make sure that management did, too. Yes, the locals would get behind this and new readers would come.

He announced the news in that day's paper. Before long countless charities approached Jim asking him to raise funds. Should he pick one or a handful? In the end he decided on a selection because the more people involved the better all round, for newspaper sales.

Recently he had stopped having lunch breaks due to sheer weight of work but forced himself to use this time to train instead. He hadn't swum for ages but a local leisure centre agreed to let him use their facilities. All good publicity. Within six weeks he'd lost a stone.

When he wasn't editing the paper or writing stories he was meeting the charities and learning about the good they did.

"Newspaper sales are increasing," reported Derek, as he strode into Jim's office one morning.

"People like good news," Jim replied. "How much are you sponsoring me, Derek?"

Derek looked away, sheepishly.

"Come on, I need your support – it's 10km for God's sake."

"Okay, okay, put me down for £250."

"That makes it more worthwhile, watching you squirm," Jim smiled. "Can you get the rest of management to put their hands in their pockets? What about corporate sponsors?"

"I'll see what I can do."

When the day arrived it was raining and the 500 contestants soon looked bedraggled at the start line. The all day event saw some stragglers finally reaching the finish line in the evening but Jim had surprised himself by coming in at a respectable 27th, completing the course in under three hours and raising more than £50,000 – the greatest achievement of any participant.

This was that day's front page lead story complete with glowing comments from all the charities that would gain as a result.

As he sat at his desk smiling at the photo of himself sprawled across the finish line, his phone rang: "What are you going to do next then?" asked Derek. "Your success is our success, we've just had the tenth newsagent reporting that they've sold out and need more copies and it's not even lunchtime yet."

TINA SHAW

At the grand age of 60, Tina Shaw graduated from Chichester University with a 2.1 degree in English and Creative Writing in 2012. Three years earlier she had fulfilled a lifelong dream to go to university. "This was something that had been on the back burner for many years," says Tina, who lives in Stubbington. "I still retain an interest in writing poetry some 10 years' later, although my prowess in writing short stories has somewhat lapsed these days."

Lost property
By Tina Shaw

Stephen, boiling with rage and resentment grasped his wife's throat. "I'll kill you," he spluttered.
Martha laughed. "Hadn't you a clue then? All those nights I went to evening classes. God you must be thick, I've spent 20 long years with you. You mean, snivelling man. I fell out of love with you

ages ago. I couldn't wait to have an affair."
She smiled as his face turned puce. "There you go again, losing your rag, you stupid man."
Stephen whirled round but pain shot through his side, up his arm. He keeled over and slithered to the ground. "Help me," he cried. But Martha had marched out of the back door. Hours later she returned to find him dead. A post mortem revealed a weak heart. Martha felt no emotion and she was relieved he was now out of her life.
Stephen's brother arrived, solicitous and brimming over with stories of how he loved Stephen more than life itself. Martha grimaced thinking, "What a load of codswallop he is spouting."
"What sort of funeral are you planning?" he asked.
"Why a humanist one of course, Stephen always wanted to be buried in Cowplain on that special burial ground. He didn't believe in God, didn't want to be cremated and years ago even bought himself a cardboard coffin. It's outside in the tool shed."
"Will it be strong enough to carry his weight?"
"Of course, it's about six feet long and he's only 5ft 8ins and he doesn't weigh that much," Martha replied. "Just leave it to me, I'll arrange everything. We can take him to the burial ground in the Volvo estate, if we collapse the seats. Don't worry, it will be fine."
Stephen's brother didn't hang around. "Well let me know what's happening, and the date of the interment. Martha waved him goodbye.
Some days later she phoned him. "It's all arranged, come to our house on Tuesday and we'll collect Stephen from the undertakers and ferry him to Cowplain ourselves. At least we'll save a bit of money that way.
Stephen's brother arrived on Tuesday. "Where's the coffin then?"
"In the kitchen. Help me carry it out will you?"
Together they staggered to the car and shoved the coffin in the boot. They set off but just as they approached Purbrook, the Volvo spluttered to a halt.
"Damn. That's the last thing I need," thought Martha. She turned to Stephen. "We'll have to take him on the bus."

c

"What, you must be kidding!"

"What else do you suggest? We have to be there by a certain time. It's the bus or nothing," said Martha. So they heaved the casket out of the Volvo and patiently waited for the bus to Cowplain. It arrived shortly. The passengers were astonished to see the coffin onboard. It caused an uproar. The conductor told them to take it upstairs because it was too upsetting. The conductor, Stephen's brother and Martha struggled, pushing, pulling and sweating profusely as they finally managed to get the heavy box upstairs. Stephen's brother and Martha propped it up against the back window and breathing a sigh of relief, sat down.

The countryside sped past and Martha relaxed. In fact she relaxed so much that she completely forgot where they were due to alight. "Oh my God we've missed our stop," she screamed. They clattered down the stairs. "Let us off," they demanded in unison. The driver looked bemused as Martha and Stephen's brother jumped off. He closed the doors and set off.

"Where's the bloody coffin – you fool?" shouted Martha.

"Oh God we forgot it – it's on the back seat! Shit." Martha sat down, her head in her hands. Stephen's brother looked horrified.

"Where does the bus go then, does it come back this way?"

"No, it continues on to Clanfield and then on to the depot in Petersfield. Heaven knows what they'll make of a coffin on board. We might as well get a taxi back to Purbrook and I'll call out the AA. In the meantime we'll cancel the funeral and phone the bus company to explain our predicament."

And that is exactly what happened. In the first instance, the bus company thought someone was playing a practical joke but on checking upstairs on the No. 88 bus, they found the coffin.

Martha arranged for the undertakers to collect it and the following day the interment went ahead. This time Martha relied on the undertakers to do all the donkey work, so Stephen's humanist burial went ahead smoothly.

TERRY WATERS

Terry Waters is 38 years old and was born in Portsmouth. He spent his life growing up in nearby Havant. "I've always had a big imagination from the first day I read my favourite book, *Around The World In 80 Days*. As a child I was often found inventing my own stories and it became my lifetime dream to have my own book published." He has a love of walking and is always thinking of others. "So in 2014 I combined the two by completing the South Downs Way Walk, with friends, for charity, by walking from Eastbourne to Winchester in four days."

Murder is easy
By Terry Waters

Dougie Meller had been lecturing on criminology at the Rose Hill University for almost twenty years. Every year had brought with it its share of gifted and not so gifted students. This year was different. This year had brought every ungifted student to his class, which wasn't necessarily a bad thing.

As it was nearing the end of the academic year and the current lecture on crime reaction in society had been dull and uninspiring, Dougie decided it was time to take advantage of his students' lack of intelligence. So as they stared mindlessly at their books, he wrote The Perfect Murder on the whiteboard. Turning back to his students he asked, "Who can tell me, what is a perfect murder?"

"When you can get away with it," shouted one of the boys, a few rows from the back, his eyes not leaving his phone. If anyone was going to shout out an answer it was the most ungifted student he had, Nick Rundel.

"Not quite…. Yes, getting away with it is part of the perfect murder but what else would make it perfect?"

Nothing but blank expressions stared back at him.

"What if no one knew it was murder?" he prompted.

"Like an accident?" questioned one of the girls from the front row. If Nick was the worst student, Claire Birch had to be head and shoulders above the rest, although she still needed to be fed half the answer before she could work out the rest.

"Let us suppose someone decided to commit a murder and make it look like an accident but there are no guarantees that the police won't find something suspicious. After all, no plan is foolproof. So, how can our murderer make sure they are not suspected in the crime?"

The blank stares continued. It was time for him to set the scene for them to work with and he had already planned this lecture in full so he knew where he wanted the class to go.

"Imagine this," he said, resting himself on the edge of his desk. "A man wants to murder his wife and knows he will be the only suspect in the crime. The police will look into every aspect of the murder, always with the husband in mind as the possible killer. Even if he does manage to set up an accident and this accident is successful in eradicating his troublesome wife, how can he be sure that he is eliminated as a possible suspect?"

"Pigs always look at the husband," scoffed Nick, crossing his feet over on the back of the seat in front of him.

"You feel the police don't have too much imagination when it comes to crime? You think they will only follow clues if they are obvious to them?"

"Well, yeah," replied Nick scornfully.

"Don't underestimate our boys in blue. Anyone who is planning a murder should always assume that the investigating officer assigned to the case is just as smart as they are. Remember, no plan is foolproof. Unless…"

"Unless what?" asked Claire, sitting forward in her seat. The whole class seemed engrossed once Dougie hinted at a foolproof plan.

"Unless our murderer has a cast iron alibi," replied Dougie, triumphantly.

The class let out a slow groan, almost like the answer had been an anticlimax to them. They were obviously expecting some words of wisdom and ended up with a cliché from mystery novels and TV programmes.

"Let us imagine this: our murderer manages to kill his wife with an accident in the home, yet at the time of the murder is giving a speech to a room full of people and has been with them most of the day. Do you think the police would suspect him of murder?"

"No, they couldn't think he had anything to do with it if he was with people the whole time." Nick looked sideways at the rest of his classmates. "Am I missing something here?"

Only a few brain cells, thought Dougie.

"Do any of you think the police would look at the husband as a viable suspect in his wife's death?"

The unanimous verdict from the class was a resounding no.

As if on cue there was a knock on the classroom door and the Dean of the university stepped into the room.

"Dean Matthews, to what do we owe this pleasure?"

"I have two police officers here to see you, Dougie," said the Dean, looking over at the students hesitantly. "You may want to speak to them in your office."

"Is there a problem?"

"It really would be best if you spoke to them in private."

"Please ask them to come in; this is a criminology lecture after all." The two CID officers walked in and repeated the Dean's words, suggesting privacy for this matter. Again Dougie refused this and asked what he could do for them. They moved closer and in hushed tones said, "It's your wife, Mr Meller…I'm afraid she had a fatal accident at home. We really would prefer to speak to you in the privacy of your office."

Dougie's mouth fell open. He looked shaken for a brief moment and composed himself.

"If you would please wait for me in my office, just down the hall, I will just excuse my class and be with you."

As the officers and the Dean left the room Dougie wiped the words from the whiteboard. He turned to look at the stunned faces of his class and with a malicious smile said, "It's that easy."

ARRON WILLIAMS

Arron Williams is a 23-year-old, aspiring author who was born in Basingstoke and has always lived there (apart from three years at university in Wales). A Master's graduate from Aston University, Arron has a background in linguistics with dedicated focus on forensics. Combining knowledge from his degrees and enthusiasm for creative writing, he enjoys blending the two to create spine shivering tales of horror and folkloric fantasy. While having spent the last eight years writing for fun in his spare time, his future plans are to move into writing and publishing books and to work on collaborative projects to produce videogames and media content, both of which are currently under development.

Colours of Frustration
By Arron Williams

A ray of crimson sweeps across the blank space. A dash of azure dotting a hazy outline. A light arc of pale sky blue. I continue to mix paint from the palette, casting my brush upon the growing colour of the once white canvas. Colours mix and merge. Patterns that run like veins, colours that burst with a grotesque blend of hues. Indigo merges to turquoise, red suddenly shifting to a blob of striking green. A resounding and defeated sigh bellowed forth from my body.

I wipe the excess, dripping fluid from the brush upon my already acrylic smeared apron. Clearing it off after another failed attempt, staring frustrated at the hideous rainbow I created. Fist clenched, I lash out. A light piercing sound of splitting, crumpling linen echoes as my throw crashes against the defenceless work. My hand swiftly recoils to reveal the result of my strike, a crushed and fractured canvas, broken inward with an unlevel cracked mark. The frustrated assault not tearing through fabric instead leaving it like a fractured eggshell. The still fresh paint simultaneously pouring into the cracks and running back out of it like a festering wound. This wound just as twisted as the failed display of pigments; the acrylic swirling and concocting new sordid arrays and shades. Although, in slight disbelief I witnessed not only the fury of my wrath but the colours splitting back from one another, colour mixing and... unmixing, in a constant transition of vibrance? Shaking my head in my frustrated state, I chalk it up to a weary mind. It was getting late after all.

My heart pounding with disappointment at the failed painting, I reach out once more, clutching the sides of the canvas as it sits upon the easel. I clasp the ruined and injured work, throwing it at the clutter of other discarded canvases that suffered a similar ruination. Once pristine and fresh, the corpses of vibrant works litter the garage floor. Sprawled out like a murder scene, others wedged against old boxes or behind workbenches. Fresh acrylic meet the old stains upon the dull red tiles of the garage floor, brightening them with smears and splotches making it look livelier. A brief glance is all I give my failed creations before storming away, closing the old door after me. I walk back under moonlight, across my garden, not looking back as I pace towards my house to call it a night. After a brief stop in the kitchen, washing my hands dry of the marks the victim's wound bled onto me, I toss the filthy apron into the sink to clean another day. Still angry, my only thought of solace being a fleeting belief that tomorrow will bring greater inspiration.

Traipsing through my small and quiet house, I head upstairs. After the classic pre-rest routine of modern man, I switch into a nightgown, ready to rest. The bedroom marked by familiar faces of perfected portraits and landscapes of sunsets on the country fields or beautiful blends of bold colours that merge to create reflections in a lake. Paintings and art crafted by the passion of youth, hands that gave life instead of a massacre.

As I crawl into bed I lay my weary head down, sinking against the pillow. My gradual descent into slumber soon cut short as the floorboards tremble, a loud sloshing resounding from outside my bedroom door. A sound like a bucket of viscous liquid swaying. "Just the pipes," I think, closing my eyes in a desperate attempt to drift off to sleep, ever hopeful that today's nightmare will end. That tomorrow's work will resemble the astute greatness of my past pieces and rocket forth my career once more. "It's what I deserve," is the only thought that crosses my mind, dwelling upon it.

The sound does not relent. Constant dripping and wet noises coming from outside the room. Without end. Opening my eyes, I gaze towards the door. Something is coming through, seeping beneath the door and through the cracks. It smears its way across the walls. I blink repeatedly. Vain hope that it is a trick of the dark. No matter how hard I try, it remains. Creeping further in through the dark. I lurch forward, slamming my hand against the bedside light switch. Attempts fumbling. Finally, a loud click. The room abruptly blasted by light, temporarily blinding me.

With my sight returning, adjusting to the light I see the thing. Now amassed in the doorway a horrific monstrosity of colour. Warped and twisted. It writhes and shifts into an endless array of sickening hues. Full of so much vibrance it is overflowing with all pigments known and unknown. Chattering jaws, vile shapes and constant indescribable appendages that form across its body. The horrifying wet noise louder now and resounding through the room as the creature closes in.

The creature; the hideous blob, draws ever closer to the bed side. Smearing and bashing the walls with awful tones of turquoise, transforming the once red walls. From its form, gnarled jaws of green teeth begin to gnash. Biting at the air like a rabid, confused animal. It isn't just the wallpaper that suffers the fate of being smeared with new tints. My pride and joy, the fiery passion of youthful work is not spared. Aquamarines and crimsons stain the once blue rivers, causing them to flood over onto the banks. The faces in the portraits struck as a slashing lash of silver strikes out, breaking the frame and gliding across the paint. Faces now marked by painful purples and twisted teals. Silver marks form pierces in the canvases. The horror, a constant shifting of hues and tones, ruining the work of youth as it draws ever nearer to me.

The God That Stole Music
By Arron Williams

When the sky was in its youth and clouds reached first bloom; there was the age of Harpies. Those who lived high above on inverse mountains that nestled upon graceful billows. They were free from the hardships below, lost amongst the boundless, never ending, azure sky. Their realm was surrounded by high flying birds, eager eagles and shy sparrows that all joined the Harpies' chorus. The grand, opulent halls full of vibrance as Harpic wings shared the feathers of all the birds in the sky.

Aeons passed, until one day Harpic culture was blessed with the arrival of three grand musicians. The first was elegant Therie, bending the very winds to her will; through a howling temperament her talons crafted the flute. The second, born of the skies grace, was Menara. She tied string to wood to create harmonic melody when plucked; the mother of lyres. The last was Meseythia, cloaked in the coat of a raven. She strayed from bloodshed grinding her talons blunt, to club and hammer her creation, the resounding beat of a drum. Together the three were elegant and beloved. They ushered a new age of music, the greatest that ever-graced mortal ears. They played and played, singing sonnets of veneration to the divine sky. Music so pure it brought peace to the realms above. The cacophony and serenade of the harmonic tunes, mixed with the thunderous applause and sounds of admiration, reached the even higher realms of the divine. Yet, none knew the tragedy to come. The Sky was thrilled, rejoicing at its children's creation, the sun and the moon danced but one divine being in its crooked form wanted the music for itself. The great god of Adoration.

It wasn't the sweetness of song that roused Adoration, but the appraisal the musicians received. They were adored by all. So, Adoration schemed, desiring the praise for itself, filled with envy that mortals were adored, without its own presence. Eventually, the time came in which Adoration chose to strike.

The musicians, led by Therie, had descended to the realms below. A rare event as harpies scarcely left the sky, but they desired to share their beautiful sound with the Elves. In the vales and valleys of the mighty Simramia kingdom that the woodland Elves called home, the harpies made their performance. Adoration skewed and warped its form becoming a vessel of a lowly elf - its divine nature disguised.

The sound filled the air and the resounding applause followed. As the praise quietened, the Elven King eager to know the origin of such unique instruments, asked jovially, "My ears writhe with splendid joy, by what ability did you weave such silky sound?" Still disguised in its humble form, all were shocked when this meek elf declared its presence. "It was mine, your grace, under my creation and patronage do these performers play." The disguised god announced.

Outraged and blinded by arrogance grown from seeing the celebration of her performance, Therie confronted the liar. "These are words of a fiend! My sisters and I crafted these sounds!" The creator of flutes protested. "We cannot prove this with words alone, a performance of skill is required to tell the true master of such profound tones!" The Elvish king declared. "Then let me and the harpy compete, with no tricks, we both use her flute," the disguised god proclaimed. The king nodded in agreement. "Therie, hand the man your flute so he may prove himself," he said gesturing for the new show to commence. "There will be no contest, I only perform with grace," claimed Therie, her talons passed the flute over.

Despite its divinity the god knew no chords or music. The mortals listened in amusement at the croaking brutish sounds. Yet their amusement blinded their awareness of the tragedy to come, distracted by the sound they were unaware that the god had blown a curse into the flute. Therie snatched it, eager to defeat the elf. She serenaded the crowd but something stirred amongst them. The audience entranced by the cursed flute; no longer resonating with the melody but beguiled to adore it. The dazed crowd joined in a prayer to Adoration, empowering the divine being.

The flautist spared no injustice as she fell into a deep trance, twisted by desire to charm others to praise Adoration. Enraged at seeing her sister tricked and entranced, Menara charged forth, lyre raised, at the god. A foolish but hopeful attempt to break the curse, the charge cut short, as her sister played once more. Struck by the sound, Menara's body contorted with strings to the form of a monstrous creature. Instruments clattered to the floor, only to be plucked from the ground by the god and added to its divine essence.

In the chaos, Meseythia covered her ears, blocking the sound. She witnessed the mutation of her sisters, no longer resembling fine musicians but creatures bound to the will of Adoration. She fled out of the vale, her drum clutched close to her chest. Adoration desperately pursued her but it was too late, Meseythia descended rapidly and reached the gates of the underworld. Knowing no other deity could pass the threshold, she pleaded with Death.

Sympathetic to her plight, Death agreed to protect her and allow her to live within the halls. To show gratitude and preserve the drum's purity, she gifted the drum to Death. Warmed, Death imbued the hearts of mortals with its beating rhythm, a symbol of life and hope as all animals large and small now felt music beyond corruption within them. All things living feeling their hearts beat. Yet, the tragedy was never forgotten. The music for all time since echoed adoration. Sorrowful, no longer do harpies or larks sing. The realm above silent; without a chorus.

FAMILY HISTORY

Record your family's voices, memories and stories now or lose them forever!

An audio file of your family history is invaluable for your children and grandchildren.

It is a comfort in times of grief while also enhancing your family tree

For more information visit:
www.**audio**ancestry.co.uk

TIM SAUNDERS PUBLICATIONS

Tim Saunders Publications specialises in great poetry and fiction.

"Everyone has a book in them," according to journalist Christopher Hitchens (1949 to 2011)

Do you have a book you would like to publish?

Email. tsaunderspubs@gmail.com

For more information visit:
tsaunderspubs.weebly.com

We are always on the look out for poetry and short stories.

THE HAMPSHIRE COLLECTION

In this book, 20 Hampshire writers contribute their poetry and short stories. There are some excellent poems including *Where we live* by Paul Franklin from Alresford and *The Lake* by Jilly Bowling from Winchester. Dan Boylan's short stories are a must-read. There's even a sprinkling of mystery, crime and fantasy. Something for everybody.

Edited by Tim Saunders, this book shines a light on contemporary writers in Hampshire, England and celebrates their talents.

Printed in Great Britain
by Amazon